Quite a long time ago, in a city called London, which is in a country called England, there lived a rich man named Ebenezer Scrooge.

Besides being rich, he was also one of the meanest, stingiest men in all of London—maybe even the stingiest in all of England, or of all the world, for that matter.

Just how mean and stingy was Ebenezer Scrooge? You'll know the answer to that when we tell you some of the things that happened one Christmas Eve.

It was late afternoon on this particular Christmas Eve. Scrooge was on his way back to his Counting House, returning with bags of money he had collected during the day.

It was very, very cold and snow was falling as he made his way down the center of the street. He could walk in the street because there was no such

WALT DISNEY PICTURES'

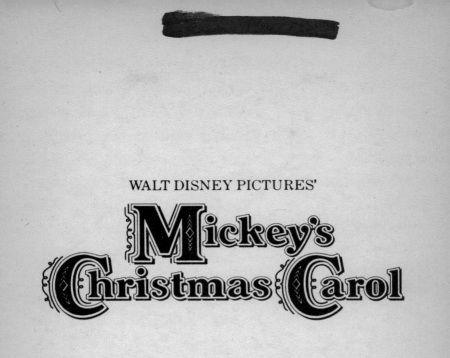

Mickey's Christmas Carol

TROLL ASSOCIATES

Mickey's Christmas Carol

thing as an automobile or even a bicycle in those days.

At the corner, a beggar cried out, "Oh, sir, give a penny—just a penny is all!"

Scrooge stopped and looked at the beggar. "Give a penny, did you say? Why should I give a penny?"

"For the poor, sir—who'll have nothing to eat on Christmas Day!" was the reply.

Scrooge slapped away the beggar's outstretched hand, and with a loud "BAH!" continued on his way.

When he reached his Counting House, he stood in front and looked up at the sign which hung over the door. "SCROOGE & MARLEY", the sign read, but the word "MARLEY" had been scratched out.

"Hah!" exclaimed Scrooge as he gazed at the sign. "Jacob Marley, my partner. It was just seven years ago today that he died. Wonderful partner, he was. He robbed old ladies and cheated the poor people. And when he died, he left me money in his will to pay for a tombstone for his grave. But I fooled him, I did! No tombstone or grave for Marley—I had him buried at sea—and kept the money for myself!"

With a harsh laugh, Scrooge opened the door of the Counting House and stepped inside. Across the room, Scrooge's clerk, Bob Cratchit, was about to put a small lump of coal into the stove, where a tiny fire was struggling to stay lit.

"CRATCHIT!" yelled Scrooge.

"Y-y-y-yes, sir?" said Cratchit, a quiet, meek young man who worked very hard for Scrooge.

"WHAT ARE YOU DOING WITH THAT LUMP OF COAL?" Scrooge shouted.

"Oh, heh-heh-heh, uh—good morning, Mr. Scrooge," stammered Cratchit. At the same time he tried to hide the

lump of coal behind his back.

"I said what are you doing with that lump of coal?" snarled Scrooge.

Cratchit was afraid to tell Scrooge he was going to put the coal on the fire, so he pretended the coal was frozen ink.

"Well, Mr. Scrooge," he began nervously, "you see, it's so cold in here that the ink froze. I was going to try to melt it in the stove!"

Scrooge, who didn't believe a word of what Cratchit said, took his cane and slashed at the lump of coal, knocking it from Bob Cratchit's hand back into the coal bucket.

"Stop giving me stupid, lying excuses!" Scrooge yelled. "Besides, you used a whole lump just last week! Now—get back to work and be quick about it!"

"Y-y-yes, sir! Right away!" Cratchit answered as he scrambled to his seat on the stool behind his high desk. Then he thought of something. "Speaking of work, Mr. Scrooge," he said, "tomorrow is Christmas. I was wondering if I could have half a day off, sir."

Scrooge, who was hanging up his hat and coat, turned with a frown.

"Christmas, eh? It's a lot of nonsense, but I suppose you could have half the day off. But I warn you—I'll *pay* you for only half a day!" Walking to his desk, Scrooge said, "Let's see now, I pay you two shillings a day. Right?"

"No, sir," Cratchit said, "it's two shillings and a half-penny, sir."

"Humph," replied Scrooge grumpily, "that's right. I gave you that raise three years ago."

"That's right, Mr. Scrooge," Cratchit said. "That was when you told me I had to do your laundry."

Scrooge was starting to empty his pockets of bags of money, then remembered something. "Very well, Cratchit—now get back to work. And here's more shirts that need laundering!" With that, he tossed a huge bundle at Cratchit and went into his office.

Almost immediately, the bell over the doorway jingled, and in walked a young man who looked like a much younger Scrooge. It was Scrooge's nephew, Fred.

"Merry Christmas!" cried Fred, as he stood in the doorway with a large Christmas wreath in his hand.

Cratchit came off his high stool to greet Scrooge's nephew.

"Merry Christmas to you, Master Fred!" he called.

At his desk, Scrooge looked up from his bags of money with a frown and a sneer. "Merry Christmas, you say? Bah, humbug, is what I say!"

Pretending not to have heard his uncle, Fred came to the door of Scrooge's office, holding the Christmas wreath.

"Merry Christmas, Uncle Scrooge," he said with a smile.

Scrooge rose from behind his desk and started to advance on Fred, who began to back away. Fred backed into Cratchit, and both stumbled and nearly fell.

"What," snarled Scrooge, "is so merry about it? I'll *tell* you what Christmas is! It's just another day to work—and anybody who doesn't think so should be pickled in his own juice!"

This upset Bob Cratchit, who said, "But, sir! Christmas is a time for giving—a time for being with your family!"

"And I say, BAH, HUMBUG!" Scrooge bellowed.

Not willing to give in to his uncle, Fred said, "I don't care what you say, Uncle Scrooge, I say Merry Christmas! A VERY Merry Christmas!"

Cratchit was so delighted with Fred's remark that he clapped his hands in

applause. "Well said, Master Fred!" he cried.

Scrooge, walking back to his office, spun around to Cratchit and said, "Cratchit! What the dickens do you think you're doing?"

Cratchit knew Scrooge was angry at him for applauding Fred, so he tried to cover up his handclapping by saying, "It's so cold in here, Mr. Scrooge—I was just beating my hands together to try to warm them a bit!"

"Humph and tommyrot!" Scrooge snorted. Then, turning to Fred, he said, "And you—what are *you* doing here, nephew?"

Fred stepped forward, handed Scrooge the Christmas wreath and said, "I've come to give you this and invite you to Christmas dinner at my house, Uncle."

Scrooge gave Fred a very strange look. Then, with an oily smile, he said, "Well, now—I suppose you'll have a nice, fat goose with chestnut dressing?"

"Yep!" said a surprised Fred.

"And you'll have plum pudding and lemon sauce?" continued Scrooge.

"We certainly will!" Fred answered.

Scrooge, holding the wreath, began to back Fred to the front door. "And you'll serve me candied fruits with spiced sugar cakes?"

"You bet!" agreed Fred. "Will you come?"

With a nasty expression on his face, Scrooge reached behind Fred and opened the front door. Fred drew back, frightened.

"Are you crazy?" Scrooge bellowed. "You know I can't eat that kind of trash!" He slammed the wreath over Fred's head, pinning his arms to his sides. He then aimed a kick at Fred, who tumbled out the door. "There's your wreath!" Scrooge cried. "Now, out—and stay out!" Then he slammed the door and walked toward his office, with another loud "BAH, HUMBUG!"

Just then, the front door opened again and Fred's head poked inside. Then his hand came around with the Christmas wreath, which he hung on the inside doorknob, he yelled, "Merry Christmas!" and slammed the door shut from the outside.

"And a BAH, HUMBUG to you!" roared Scrooge.

Cratchit, behind his desk, chuckled to himself and said aloud, "That Fred! He's always so full of kindness!"

Scrooge replied, "Yeah. He was always peculiar—and stubborn, too!"

A few minutes later, the doorbell rang once more and two men walked into the Counting House. Scrooge looked up, rubbed his hands in delight and said, "Well, well, well—I do believe we have customers!" Then he waved at his clerk and said, "I'll handle this, Cratchit." Walking toward the two men he smiled and said, "Well, now—what

can I do for you two fine gentlemen this fine day?"

The first man spoke up. "We, sir, are soliciting funds for the indigent and destitute."

Scrooge's smile turned into a scowl. "You're doing *what* for *who*?" he howled.

The second man removed his hat and held out a cup to Scrooge. "We're collecting money for the poor," he explained.

Scrooge then showed just how mean and stingy he could be. Smiling his nasty, oily smile, he said, "Well, now. Let's think about this a little. Suppose I give you a sum of money to give to the poor."

The second man began to get happily excited. "Oh, yes, sir!" he said. "That would be wonderful!"

"Just one minute," continued Scrooge. "If I do that, and you give the money to them—then they won't be poor anymore, will they?"

"Well, I don't know about—" began the first man.

"Hush!" ordered Scrooge. "And if they're not poor anymore, then you won't have to raise money for them anymore. Am I correct?"

The second man said, "But you were going to—"

"Just a minute!" interrupted

Scrooge. "Now—if you didn't have to raise money for the poor anymore, you'd be out of a job, wouldn't you?" All the while he was saying this, he was moving toward the front door, shoving the two men in front of him. He then opened the door and exclaimed, "Please, please, don't ask me to put you out of a job on Christmas Eve! He gave one final shove and shouted, "Out! Out! And don't come back!"

After slamming the door, Scrooge leaned back against it and said, "This is a very strange world, Cratchit." He started for his office, talking as he went. "I work hard all the time for my money! Why do people think I will give it away to anybody?"

While Scrooge was talking, the clock on the wall was striking. When it stopped at seven, Cratchit slid off his stool, and began to get ready to leave.

In his office, Scrooge looked at his watch. Speaking loud enough for Cratchit to hear, Scrooge said,

"Hmmm. Clock's two minutes fast."

With a sigh, Cratchit climbed back on his stool and started to work again. However, just then Scrooge said, "Well, never mind the two minutes. You may go now."

Cratchit jumped off his stool again and said, "Oh, thank you, sir! You're so kind!"

"Never mind that mushy stuff!" exclaimed Scrooge. "Just go—but be here all the earlier the next day!"

Cratchit picked up the bag of laundry and started out the door, headed for home.

Over an hour later, Scrooge decided he'd counted enough money for one day. He stretched, sighed once or twice, then put on his hat, coat, scarf and gloves and he, too, went out the door and headed for home.

He mounted the steps to his front door, upon which was nailed a door-knocker in the shape of a lion's head.

But as he reached for the door knob, something strange seemed to be happening to the lion's head. As he watched, it seemed to him that it began to look like his old, long-dead partner, Jacob Marley! And then he thought he heard the head moan, "S-C-R-O-O-O-O-O-G-E!"

"Marley? Jacob Marley?" muttered Scrooge to himself. "No! That can't be! He's dead—dead these seven years!"

Then the knocker seemed to groan his name once more. Scrooge was really scared this time and ran into the house. As he climbed the stairs, he thought he heard something that sounded like footsteps and chains rattling behind him. However, every time he took a quick look back down the stairs, he saw nothing at all. Finally he said, "Bah! I must have eaten something that disagreed with me. I'm hearing things, that's all." And then he heard the rattling of heavy chains *again*—but still could see nothing when he looked around. Scrooge shook his head, said, "Bah, humbug!" once and then ran up the stairs as fast as he could, got to his bedroom door, opened it, went inside, slammed the door shut and bolted and locked it.

He went to his big armchair and sat down. "Phew!" he said. "I sure wish I knew what that noise was on the stairs. Oh, well—maybe I'm hearing things—nothing to worry about, I guess—WHAT'S THAT?!!!"

'THAT' was the clanking noise of chains again. As Scrooge stared at the door, his eyes popped wide as he watched a shadowy figure coming *through* the door!

"Oh, no!" groaned Scrooge. Then, as the figure began to take shape, he groaned again. "Impossible!" he moaned. "It can't be!" By that time, the figure was standing in front of Scrooge—and Scrooge knew who it was!

"Marley! Jacob Marley!" Scrooge's mouth was so dry from fright that he could hardly talk.

"That's right," said the figure. "Jacob Marley himself—your old partner!"

"But, Jacob—you're dead—dead for seven long years—and besides that, I can see right through you!"

"Oh, Ebenezer," the figure said. "You always were very clever about money matters, but a little stupid about other things. Of course, you can see through me—I'm a ghost!"

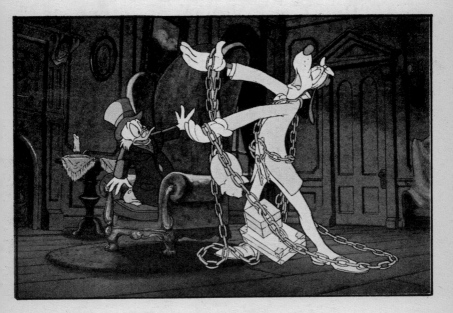

"What," demanded Scrooge, "are you doing here—and what do you want with *me*?"

Marley rattled his chains again, and then said, "Ebenezer, remember how I robbed old ladies, and cheated the poor people?"

"Of course I remember," Scrooge replied. "You were very good at it! You were almost as good as I was—and still am!"

"Oh, I was good, all right," Marley said. "But I was *wrong*—as wrong as wrong can be!"

"What do you mean, Jacob?" Scrooge asked.

"I mean just this, Ebenezer," Marley went on. "You see these heavy chains?"

"Of course I see them!" snapped Scrooge. "You think I'm blind? And by the way, why do you keep dragging them around? Aren't they very heavy?"

"They are *terribly* heavy," replied Marley. "And I keep dragging them around because I *have* to. They're my punishment for all the nasty, mean things I did when I was alive!"

"G-g-gosh!" stammered Scrooge. "How long will you have to keep doing it?"

"Forever," Marley said. "Maybe even longer! That's why I've come here tonight, Ebenezer."

"W-w-why is that?" Scrooge asked nervously.

"To warn you!" Marley said. "There's no hope for me—the weight of these chains will always be with me. But it's not too late for you, Scrooge—*if* you change your ways!"

"How?" Scrooge yelped. "Help me, Jacob! Tell me how!"

"Very well, Ebenezer," Marley replied. "This is your chance—and probably your *last* one. Tonight you will be visited by three spirits. Listen to what they have to say. Do as they tell you—because if you don't—your chains will be even heavier than mine! Farewell, Scrooge—remember what I told you!"

As he said "Farewell," the ghost of Marley began to fade. By the time he finished saying, "Remember what I told you," he had disappeared completely.

Scrooge sat in his chair for a few minutes, then rose to his feet, saying, "Marley, eh? Dead for seven years—and trying to frighten *me*—Ebenezer Scrooge? Hah! Three spirits coming to call, eh? Pooh! Spirits? I say bah, humbug to Marley and his spirits and Christmas, too!" And with that, he undressed, put on his night clothes and got into bed. The bed was quite a big one, with curtains all around to help keep out the light and the winter's cold air. In a few minutes, Scrooge was sound asleep and snoring.

He slept for about an hour, then was awakened by the "Ding! Ding! Ding!" of his bedside alarm clock. Scrooge rolled over, opened one eye and grunted, "It can't be morning already. I must have imagined I heard the clock!"

In a few seconds he was snoring once more, but again came the "Ding! Ding! Ding!"

"What the—" sputtered Scrooge. "It *is* the clock—but what's going on? It's still the middle of the night!"

He poked open the curtains and looked around. There, on his night table, was a tiny creature which looked like a cricket. The creature was tapping its foot impatiently.

"Well!" said the tiny one. "It's about time! I don't like to be kept waiting—haven't got all night, y' know!"

"Ulp!" gasped Scrooge. "Who—who are you?"

"Silly!" exclaimed the creature, pointing to a badge he was wearing.

29

"I'm the Spirit of Christmas Past!"

"Oh," Scrooge said. "But you're—"

"I'm *what*?" said the Spirit. "Speak up, Scrooge!"

"Oh—yes—certainly," Scrooge said. "It's just that I thought you'd be maybe somewhat taller!"

"Size has nothing to do with it!" snapped the Spirit. "Let me tell you something, Scrooge. If size were measured by kindness—you'd be smaller than a speck of dust in the air!"

"Well," murmured Scrooge as he pulled his blanket up, lay back and prepared to go to sleep again, "kindness never got *me* anywhere. No, sir! You can have kindness. I'll just look out for myself first, last and always!"

"Let me tell you something, Scrooge," said the Spirit. "You didn't always think so. C'mon—out of bed! It's time to go!"

"That's fine with me!" Scrooge growled. "Go!"

The Spirit hopped up on the window ledge and straining, managed to open the window. Outside, the wind blew and the snow whirled, some of it drifting into the room.

"Hey!" yelled Scrooge, holding onto the blanket, which was flapping in the wind. "What the heck do you think you're doing?"

Pointing with his umbrella out the window and holding onto his hat, the Spirit cried, "We're going to pay a visit to your past!"

Scrooge walked to the window and shouted, "Not me! You're not going to get me to go out there in my nightshirt in this weather!"

The Spirit said, "Stop arguing with me, Scrooge! Hold out your hand!"

Scrooge held out his hand and the Spirit hopped into it, then raised his umbrella. "Just hold on to me!" he ordered. "Not too tight, though!"

Suddenly, Scrooge felt himself begin

to lift off the floor. "I'm not going out there!" he screamed. "I'll fall!"

"Oh, hush!" said the Spirit. "Here we go!"

And then—they were out of the window into the night and the wind and the snow, flying high over the rooftops of London.

"Yeowwww!" screamed Scrooge.

"What's the matter, Scrooge?" said the Spirit. "Don't you like the nice, cold, crisp, blowing, freezing night air? Very well, let's go down a bit."

As they flew lower and lower, Scrooge suddenly said, "Spirit, that shop over there—I believe I know it!"

A few moments later they stood outside of a shop. Over the big window, a sign read, FEZZIWIG TEA CO. Scrooge dashed to the window and looked in. "By golly, it's old Fezziwig's place, all right! What a wonderful person he was! I couldn't have worked for a nicer, kinder man!"

Looking in the window, the Spirit and Scrooge could see a figure seated on a high desk, playing a merry tune on a violin for a crowd of people.

"Good heavens!" exclaimed Scrooge. "It's old Fezziwig himself! And they're all old friends of mine from a long time ago. And there, over in the corner—you see that shy young man all by himself? Well, that's me—a long, long time ago!"

"Yes, that was you, all right!" agreed the Spirit. "Only that was before you became such a miserable, mean, nasty, stingy old man!"

"Well," said Scrooge, "nobody's perfect, y'know! But look there—you see that pretty girl standing in the middle of the room? That's my Isabel! How beautiful she looks!"

Inside, Isabel walked over to Scrooge, took him by the hand and led him to the center of the room. "Ebenezer," she said, "my eyes are closed, my lips are ready, I'm standing under the mistletoe

and I'm waiting for you to kiss me!"

"Silly!" said Isabel, and kissed young Scrooge.

Outside the window, Scrooge said, "I remember how much I was in love with her."

"Yes," replied the Spirit, "but by ten years later, you loved something else even more!"

Suddenly, Fezziwig's Tea Co. disappeared and Scrooge and the Spirit were outside of another window.

"Migosh!" gasped Scrooge. "It's my Counting House!"

"Look in the window, Scrooge," ordered the Spirit.

Scrooge peered into the window. He could see his desk, with stacks of money piled upon it. Behind the stacks of money, Scrooge was counting.

"Nine thousand, nine hundred and seventy-two, nine thousand, nine hundred and seventy-three—"

Just then the front door opened and Isabel walked in. "Ebenezer," she began.

"Yes, yes—what is it?" said an impatient Scrooge.

"For many years," continued Isabel, "I've had this lovely cottage. It's perfect for a honeymoon and for us to live in forever. I've been waiting all these years for you to keep your promise to marry me."

Behind the pile of money, Scrooge finished stacking coins.

"I must know, Ebenezer," Isabel said. "Have you decided?"

Scrooge smacked his fist into the palm of his hand. "Yes," he said, "I have! When you wanted to buy this cottage of yours, you came to me to borrow the money to pay for it. You promised to pay back the money by making a payment by 12 o'clock noon on the first day of every month. Your final payment, Isabel, arrived on the first of the month at 1 p.m.—one hour late. You failed to live up to our agreement, Isabel, and the house now belongs to me. I'll thank you to be out of there by tomorrow—I have someone who will pay me a lot of money to rent it!"

Outside the Counting House, the Spirit said, "You see, Scrooge? You loved your money more than that won-

derful girl—and you lost her forever!"

Inside, Scrooge was behind his desk, counting again. "Nine thousand, nine hundred and seventy-four—"

And outside, Scrooge wailed, "Spirit, I cannot bear these memories. Take me home!"

"Remember, Scrooge," replied the cricket-like Spirit, "those are *your* memories—you made them yourself! Good-bye!"

The next thing that Scrooge heard was the clock on the side of his bed striking two o'clock. He sat up in bed and began to moan to himself about all his past foolishness, when he noticed that there seemed to be a lot of light outside of his curtained bed. He leaned over and peeked out.

"Wha-wha-wha-WHAT!" he yelled.

Sitting in Scrooge's big chair was a person—but what a person! He was so big you'd have to call him a giant. Surrounding him were plates, platters, tables and chests, all of which were *covered* with giant-sized food. The whole room was brilliantly lit, but Scrooge couldn't see where the light was coming from.

The giant looked at Scrooge's head, which was poked through the bed-curtains.

"A-ha!" said the giant, in a voice which was as big as he was. "Fee, fi—" At this point, Ebenezer Scrooge ducked back inside the curtains.

The giant began again. "Fee, fi, fo, fum, I smell a stingy Englishman!"

Scrooge pulled open the curtains to see the enormous eye of the giant looking at him. The giant then reached inside, and plucked Scrooge out, held him up and sniffed at him.

"I think I do," he said, and sniffed again. "Yes, I do!"

"Please, Mr. Giant!" Scrooge begged. "Don't eat me!"

"Eat you?" laughed the giant. "Why would the Spirit of Christmas Present—that's me—want to eat a very bad-tasting meanie like you? There are far better things to eat in this world!"

The giant held Scrooge up in his fingers, then moved him in the air across the room past all the good things to eat piled around the room.

"Wh-where did all this food come from?" gasped Scrooge.

"This," said the giant, "is the food of

generosity, which you have never, ever displayed to anyone in this world."

"Generosity?" cried Scrooge. "Bah! Nobody ever was generous with me!"

"You never gave anyone reason to be," declared the giant. "And yet—as mean, and stingy and nasty as you are, there are some who wish you well. Not many, mind you—but there are still a few!"

"Hah! No one that I know well, I'll bet!" Scrooge growled.

The giant slid Scrooge into the pocket of his coat. "Don't believe anything anybody says, huh? Well—we'll just have a look and maybe you'll be convinced."

The giant stood up, pushed with one hand, and lifted the roof off of Scrooge's house. He stepped into the street, replacing the roof as he did so, and began to walk through the streets of London. A few giant steps later, he lay down in the snow and peered into the window of

a small house. He then lifted Scrooge from his pocket, saying, "Okay, Scrooge, here we are. Have a look!"

Scrooge said, "What sort of stupid nonsense is this? Why did you bring me to this old shack of a house? ULP!"

The ULP! was Scrooge's exclamation of surprise as he recognized the persons in the house.

"Yes, Scrooge, this old shack, as you choose to call it, is the home of your overworked and underpaid employee, Bob Cratchit!"

Inside the house, Bob Cratchit and two of the children were trimming a very small Christmas tree, watched by Mrs. Cratchit, who was busily preparing a meal. She pulled a platter from the stove and removed the lid.

"For goodness sake!" Scrooge exclaimed. "Is that going to be Christmas dinner for the family? It looks like she's cooked a canary! Surely they have more food than that!" He paused, looking

around the room. "There! I knew it!
That big pot on the fire!"

The giant looked and said, "That's
your laundry being boiled, Scrooge!"

Mrs. Cratchit set the platter with the
tiny bird on it on the table. The two
children began to jump up and down
with excitement, and came running to
the table. The boy jumped on a chair
and tied a napkin around his neck.

Bob Cratchit said, "Not yet, children—we must wait for Tiny Tim."

From upstairs, a small voice called, "Coming, Father!" And a moment or two later, Tiny Tim came down the stairs, leaning heavily on his small crutch. His father picked him up and sat him in his chair at the table.

"Oh!" exclaimed Tiny Tim. "Look at all the wonderful things to eat." He put down his knife and fork and said, "We must give thanks to Mr. Scrooge."

"Spirit," said Scrooge, "what's wrong with that boy—the one who uses a crutch?"

"A lot of things, I'm afraid. If things don't change," the giant continued, "there will be an empty chair at Tiny Tim's place. And very soon, I'm afraid."

Scrooge said, "Then that means Tim will—help! Where'd he go? Spirit! What happened?" Suddenly, Cratchit's house disappeared in a cloud of smoke. "Spirit! Don't go! I must know about Tim! Don't go, Spirit, I beg you!"

The smoke began to clear. When Scrooge could see again, he found himself leaning on a gravestone. He jumped back in surprise and fright, then grew even more frightened when he saw the next spirit. "Who-who-who are you?" he gasped. When the Spirit merely looked sadly at him, he continued, "Are you the Spirit of Christmas Future?"

The Spirit pointed to a little group of people gathered around a grave. Scrooge said, "Please—please speak to me! Tell me—what will happen to Tiny Tim?"

Once again the Spirit pointed to the group of people. This time, Scrooge peered more closely at them. He exclaimed, "Good heavens! It's Bob and Mrs. Cratchit and two children—but where's Tiny Tim?" He watched in horror as Bob Cratchit, holding Tiny Tim's crutch, placed it against a gravestone.

"Oh, no!" groaned Scrooge, as

Cratchit turned and joined his little family.

"Spirit," Scrooge said, "this should not have happened to that brave young boy! I didn't *want* it to happen! Tell me—can't this be changed? If I could only—" He interrupted himself as he heard laughter from a nearby grave, where two gravediggers were at work.

The first gravedigger laughed again and said, "I've never, ever seen a funeral like this one."

The second digger said, "Me, either. Not a mourner, not a friend to say good-bye to him. Not one, single, solitary person. Boy, how people must have hated him when he was alive!"

The first digger said, "Let's move away from here and rest a bit. I'm tired."

"Me, too," agreed the second digger. As they moved off, Scrooge whispered to the Spirit, "What an unpleasant per-

son he must have been! Tell me, Spirit—whose lonely grave is this?"

The Spirit moved to the grave as Scrooge followed. Then the Spirit lit a match. Scrooge looked closely at the gravestone, then gasped as he read the name.

"Yes, Ebenezer Scrooge," the Spirit said, "it's *your* grave. You'll probably be the richest man in the cemetery—but with not one single person to care about you."

"N-n-n-no!" shouted Scrooge. "I won't! This is not right! I can change! I *will* change. Spirit! You *must* give me another chance! I can do so many good things if you'll only—" He had to stop, as clouds of smoke rose around him again and the entire grave-yard—diggers, Cratchits, Spirit and gravestones disappeared in the smoke.

"Wha-wha-what happened?" Scrooge muttered as he looked around as the smoke cleared. Then he knew where he was.

"How about that?" he said. "I'm back in my own bed, in my own house!" Then he poked his head through the opening in the curtains and blinked at the brilliant sunshine pouring into the room. In the distance, he could hear church bells.

Almost leaping out of the bed, he dashed to the window and gazed about him. Some fresh snow had fallen during the night, and it seemed as if everything in sight was covered with a beautiful white blanket.

"Hurrah!" shouted Scrooge. "It's Christmas morning! I haven't missed out! Those wonderful spirits did the whole thing in just one night! I've got another chance!"

In a hurry, Scrooge threw on his jacket and hat, singing merrily as he did so. "Oh, whoop-te-do, so much to do!" he sang.

"Lots of money—need plenty of money," he laughed. Then he said, "I know what I'll do—and who I'll do it to! Hey! That's a pretty good rhyme, Ebenezer!"

He picked up his scarf as he rushed out the door. He started down the stairs still laughing. Suddenly he remembered—he couldn't go out like that! He forgot something!! He rushed back up the stairs, threw open the door and grabbed his cane. "There! That's better!" he shouted, slamming the door.

He was so happy he never even

noticed that he forgot his vest and spats. He didn't even notice that he still had on his nightshirt and slippers. He was so happy he just wanted to wish everyone he saw a merry Christmas. He was so happy that he wanted everyone else to be happy too! He was *so happy* he felt as though he should give everyone some of his money!

Laughing and singing he hurried down his front steps. He made his way through the streets shouting, "Merry Christmas! Merry Christmas to one and all" to everyone he met. This caused quite a few surprised looks—as the mean, stingy, nasty Ebenezer Scrooge walked happily and merrily to his Counting House, shouting greetings as he went.

Once in the Counting House, he put bag after bag of money in every pocket, then locked the door and went out into the street once more.

Still crying, "Merry Christmas to one and all!" to everyone in sight, he came upon the beggars he had passed the evening before.

"Sir, please, give a penny for food this Christmas day!" wailed the beggar. Then, seeing who he had spoken to, the beggar pulled back and whined, "Sorry, guvnor, didn't see who you were at first!"

"NONSENSE!" roared Scrooge. "What do you mean, you miserable villain! Give a penny, indeed!"

"Sorry, guvnor!" pleaded the beggar. "Don't mean any harm—just trying to—"

"NONSENSE!" roared Scrooge once more, this time louder than before. "What can you buy with a penny, you fool? Here! You need plenty of money! Take this! And take more for your friends on the other corners!" With that, he pulled out four bags of money and handed them to the beggar, at the same time shouting, "Merry Christmas! Merry Christmas! What a wonderful day! Ha! Ha! Hee! Hee! And I'll get it all done—just wait and see!"

As he moved down the street, he saw, coming towards him, the two men who had asked him to give money for the poor when they visited him in his Counting House on Christmas Eve.

He stood in the street, with a frowning, scowling face as the two approached. When they caught sight of him, they stopped and began to back away.

"Oh, no you don't!" yelled Scrooge. "You're not going to get away from me this time! Come here!"

The two men approached Scrooge slowly, not knowing what to expect, but really afraid of Scrooge.

"Are you two still trying to get honest, hardworking people to give money so that people who don't work can live without being hungry all the time?" he thundered.

"Uh-uh-why, yes, I guess—uh, no, not really, but then we must ask for—" the first man stammered.

"Speak up!" Scrooge bellowed. "Are you or aren't you trying to raise money for the unfortunate poor?"

"Uh—I suppose—well, yes, since you put it that way," the second man replied. As he did, the first man moved behind him, trying to hide.

Scrooge reached into his coat pocket and pulled out a bag full of gold coins. "Here!" he said. "Will this do to get you started?" He handed the bag to the second man, who opened it and looked inside. "Goodness!" he exclaimed. "Must be fifty gold pieces in there!"

"What! Not enough?" Scrooge cried. "Here! Take another! Take two more! And make sure those poor people have a good meal! It's Christmas, you know! Merry Christmas!" With that, he

started off down the street once more. The two men just stared at Scrooge as he moved away, then finally shouted, "Thank you! Thank you, Mr. Scrooge!"

Scrooge hadn't gone very far when a horse-drawn wagon came into view. Driving the wagon was his nephew, Fred. "Ho, there, Fred!" Scrooge exclaimed. "Merry Christmas!" Fred was so surprised he stopped the horse in a hurry—so much in a hurry that he slid off the seat of the wagon into the horse's neck!

"I'm expecting a great meal at your house this afternoon, nephew!" he called.

"You mean you're *coming*?" Fred said.

"Coming? Of course I'm coming—you know how much I like candied fruits with spiced sugar cakes! Two o'clock sharp! I'll be there!" And with that, he got going down the street again. "Now!" he exclaimed to himself. "Now for the Cratchits!"

He made two stops along the way. At the first stop, his purchases went into a large bag. At the second, he added many more to the bag's contents.

He rapped sharply with his cane on the Cratchit's front door. "Open up in there!" he yelled.

The door was opened, and Bob Cratchit stood there, looking surprised at his visitor.

"Why, Mr. Scrooge!" he said. Then he added a timid, "M-m-m-merry Christmas!"

Scrooge charged into the house. Then he turned on Bob Cratchit, who was following him. "Merry Christmas, is it?" he roared. "Bah, humbug! I've brought another bundle for you!" He deposited his bag under the Cratchit's Christmas tree.

Bob Cratchit looked completely unhappy at this. "More laundry?" he said. "But, Mr. Scrooge—it's Christmas Day!"

"Ah-hah!" Scrooge yelled. "Christmas—one more excuse for being lazy! And another thing, Cratchit—I've had enough of this half-day off I was fool enough to give you! You leave me no choice—I'm going to give you—" Then he opened the bag under the tree and slid it toward Tiny Tim. Then he finished the sentence—"toys!"

"Toys!" shouted Tiny Tim and the other children. "Toys?" cried Bob and Mrs. Cratchit.

"Yes, toys!" Scrooge declared. "And a few other things. At the bottom of the bag is the biggest turkey I could find!"

"Wow!" yelled Bob Cratchit. "A *whole* turkey?"

"Of course, a *whole* turkey!" Scrooge said. "Turkeys don't come in pieces! And besides that, I'm giving you a raise—and making you my partner!"

"Your p-p-partner?" said Bob Cratchit.

"Yes, my partner!" Scrooge said. "And stop repeating everything I say!" He picked up Tiny Tim, smiled and said, "Merry, merry Christmas, Cratchits!" Then he put Tiny Tim down gently, went to the door, said, "Merry Christmas!" once more—and was gone.

Then Tiny Tim added the thought that was in all their minds and hearts.

"God bless us, every one!"